Published by Ladybird Books Ltd.
A Penguin Company
Penguin Books Ltd., 80 Strand London WC2R 0RL
Penguin Books Australia Ltd., Camberwell, Victoria, Australia
Penguin Books (NZ) Ltd., Private Bag 102902, NSMC, Auckland, New Zealand

2 4 6 8 10 9 7 5 3 1

LADYBIRD and the device of a ladybird are trademarks of Ladybird Books Ltd.

Printed in Italy
www.ladybird.co.uk

DISNEY's
HOME
On The
RANGE

Ladybird

Long ago in the wild, wild West, there was a little Patch of Heaven. It was a farm – home to a bunch of lively animals and its owner Pearl. She loved her place and every animal on it.

6

Pearl's two dairy cows, Mrs Caloway, the older leader of the farm animals, and Grace, the younger cow, were about to be joined by one more cow…

"Everybody, this here is Maggie," Pearl announced. Maggie was coming to live on the farm. An outlaw had stolen all the other cattle on Maggie's ranch, leaving the owner penniless – and Maggie homeless.

"Whoa, Buck! Take it easy!" yelled Sheriff Brown, as he galloped onto Pearl's farm on his fame-hungry horse.

As the dust settled, the sheriff handed Pearl a letter from the bank. Patch of Heaven was going to be sold at auction in three days' time… unless Pearl could pay up. But the farmer just didn't have the money.

"I'm sorry, girls," she told the cows.
"I'm just plum outta ideas."

Maggie, however, wasn't ready to lose another home. The county fair was only a few weeks away and Maggie was a blue-ribbon winner. She figured she could win enough prize money to pay the bank the money they owed. They just needed to have a talk with Buck to ask for a little more time.

The cows found Buck showing off as usual. He laughed at their plans. "Your farm is history," he told them. Pearl owed $750, much more than the cows could ever win.

Suddenly, swirling clouds of dust darkened the main street as a shadowy figure rode into town.

"Rico!" gasped Buck. The bounty-hunter had rounded up every no-good varmint in the West – except one. Alameda Slim was next on his list. And there was a bounty of $750 on his head.

"I'm gonna need a fresh horse," Rico announced.

Buck sprang into action and did as many fancy tricks as he could to impress Rico. It worked. Rico saddled Buck up and prepared to hunt down Alameda Slim.

Maggie's eyes opened wide when she heard this. "Why don't we go nab that Alameda Slim and use the reward money to save the farm?" she asked.

In no time, the cows found themselves tied to the back of a chuck wagon on the way to a nearby cattle drive. Where there were cattle, Maggie figured, sooner or later Slim would show his face.

That night, the cows joined up with the cattle drive. Almost at once, a shot rang through the darkness. It was Alameda Slim, and he was making his move!

Maggie didn't waste any time. "Come on, girls! Time to lose these ropes," Maggie said. She charged Slim as soon as she saw him – until something stopped her in her tracks. It was Slim yodelling! The horrible sound hypnotised the herd and the bounty-hunting cows. So that was how Slim stole so many cattle!

14

Luckily Grace was completely tone-deaf, so Slim's music had no effect on her. She had to rescue her friends.

Grace, still attached to the wagon, just managed to scoop up Maggie and Mrs Caloway when the wagon sped alongside them. But now they were out of control!

15

The cows ran smack into Rico and Buck! Buck was determined to be a hero. But he was showing off to the cows so much that Rico thought he was crazy and decided to get another horse. Shocked, Buck decided to set off after Slim by himself.

It was hard to follow Slim's tracks. To make matters worse, the heavens opened and rain poured down. Suddenly, a raging flash flood swept the cows away. Only Mrs Caloway's quick wits saved Maggie, but the cows quarrelled and were soon as miserable as the weather.

Out on the prairie, a rain-soaked
Buck was ready to give up and go
home – until he spotted a poster
of Alameda Slim. With his hopes
of being a hero raised again, Buck
galloped off.

Deep in his hideout, Alameda Slim showed his gang, the Willies, his secret disguise. Dressed as rich banker Yancy O'Del, he was determined to buy up all the farms for miles around. And the Patch of Heaven was his next target.

BEAZLEY
BEND

RIVER
BEND

MIKE
JNALD

DIXON
RANCH

PATCH
OF
HEAVEN

FINCH
ACRES

MAN
HILLS

The next morning, there was still coolness between the cows.

But almost at once, they had a piece of luck. They met a peg-legged, scorpion eating rabbit called Lucky Jack!

Lucky Jack let slip that his old home in Echo Mine had been taken over by an outlaw. "There he is!" cried Lucky Jack, spotting a poster of Alameda Slim.

"You mean this no-good varmint is hiding out in Echo Mine right now?" gasped Maggie. She needed the other cows on her side. "The three of us go together, and we're sure to get him. Once you collect the reward, I'll walk out your front gate and stay out," she promised.

"Deal!" said Mrs Caloway.

When the cows turned up at the mine, Junior was guarding the entrance. Buck was there too, trying to talk his way in.

"Cows only," said Slim's buffalo firmly. The girls strolled past, taking Lucky Jack with them.

In the mine, a Mr Wesley had arrived by train to pay for the cattle. Maggie quickly thought of a plan to capture Slim. "You two get his attention while I sneak up behind him and knock him into the cart," she said. "Then we rope him up and wheel him to justice!"

Outside, Buck had plans of his own. He conned Rico's new horse into heading for the hills.

Back in the mine, everything happened very fast. Grace popped bits of Lucky Jack's fluffy tail into her friends' ears. Slim couldn't understand why his yodelling wasn't working and walked right into Maggie's trap. "Ooooh!" he yelled as Maggie shoved the cart under him and Jack tied his hands and feet.

"Let's get outta here!" shouted Grace, as the Willies dashed to help their leader.

"Watch out!" cried Jack. Rushing to escape, the cows ran smack into Buck.

"I got Slim!" squealed the horse, hardly believing his luck. He zoomed his captive outside to Rico only to lose him again to the fast-acting cows.

A wild chase through the mine followed. Up! Down! Through tunnels! Wesley, Buck and the Willies chased our heroes.

Suddenly, sparks from the cart's wheels exploded gunpowder and dynamite in the mine. KABOOM! The cows, Slim and the cart were blown right outside and down the mountain onto the train tracks below.

"We made it, girls!" cried Maggie.

But round the bend sped the cattle train. It was heading straight for them!

CRASH! As the smoke cleared, the Willies tied up the cows. And then there was an even bigger shock in store. Rico wasn't a hero at all! He was Slim's partner in crime. Laughing, Slim rode off to buy Patch of Heaven. Buck suddenly realised who the good guys really were.

The cows were trapped on the train, but Buck urged them on. Free at last, they decided to drive the train right into Patch of Heaven.

"It… it can't be!" cried Slim, in his Y. O'Del disguise, as the cows strode towards him. He drew his gun, but the farm animals were faster. Tin cans whizzed through the air. "Ah! Ooh! Ouch!" yelled the outlaw.

The sheriff grinned. "Alameda Slim, you're under arrest!"

"Woo-eee!" cried Pearl. "My farm is saved!"

And Maggie? Did she walk off into the sunset? No, sirree! She and the other animals became famous all over the West, and Patch of Heaven became her home on the range forever.